Style Patrol

by Maria Neuman

S0-BZW-856

SCHOLASTIC INC.

New York   Toronto   London   Auckland   Sydney

Mexico City   New Delhi   Hong Kong   Buenos Aires

ISBN 0-439-70006-X

TROLLZ and its logo and all related characters
TM & © 2005 DIC Entertainment, under license from DAM.
All Rights Reserved.

Published by Scholastic Inc.
SCHOLASTIC and associated logos are trademarks
and/or registered trademarks of Scholastic Inc.
Cover design by Pamela Darcy
Interior design by Louise Bova

12 11 10 9 8 7 6 5 4 3 2 1   5 6 7 8 9 10/0

Printed in China.
First printing, October 2005

Are you ready to get seriously styling?

Sometimes getting dressed isn't so easy. Every girl has had one of those days when she tries on twelve outfits before leaving for school and none of them seem to work. Well, Amethyst, Onyx, Ruby, Sapphire, and Topaz are about to solve all of your dressing dilemmas. This little pink book is full of everything you'll need to figure out your inner troll style type. From tips and quizzes to fresh and funky do-it-yourself style ideas, your friends the trollz will help you figure out what you should wear, when to wear it, and what trends fit your personality best.

Are you ready to get hair-to-toe glamorized, trendified, stylized, and trollified? Well, what are you waiting for? Turn the page and let's go!

The Ultimate Style Gemification Guide

*W*ant to know more about your personality and get an insight into your style choices? Easy! Just check out the different trollz and their corresponding stones, and pick the colored gem that's your favorite. Now read all about yourself and learn how to work some trollz style into your life.

Your Personality: If there were a "best friend" award, you would win it. Your personality is totally easygoing and good-hearted.

Your Style: You like to keep it simple with a few feminine pieces that all go together. That way, you can make tons of outfits with a couple of key pieces.

AMETHYST

To Try: Since your warm personality draws people to you, why not stand out occasionally with a bold statement? Try to wear one bold item every day, like a pendant in your own personal signature symbol. Amethyst's fave symbol is the heart.

Your Personality: You are the trollzaniest of all gems, and you're blessed with a creative brain that can think of more ideas in five minutes than other people could in a week. This might make you a bit of a daydreamer, so try jotting down some "to do" lists every day.

TOPAZ

Your Style: One of the ways you express your creativity is through your clothes, so you're definitely someone who sets trends instead of following them.

To Try: You're a fashion natural, so sewing your own designs would be a fab creative outlet.

Your Personality: You look totally cool on the outside, but you have a heart of gold. You're a little bit of a rebel and you're always quick with a funny quip or comeback. You have a talent for getting to the truth of any situation.

ONYX

Your Style: You like to walk on the dark side when it comes to style. Your preference for colors like dark purple, magenta, and black is just your special flare for drama.

To Try: Learn how to lighten up a little bit. It's flattering to wear a soft color around your face, such as a sky blue or heather gray.

Your Personality: You are a born leader and like to be the center of attention. People can think you are strong-willed, but your close friends know that deep down you are very kind.

RUBY

Your Style: You don't usually spend a ton of time deciding what to wear, but you still like to make a style statement with bright colors.

To Try: Don't get stuck in a style rut of jeans and funky T's—show your feminine side with a skirt or cute flats.

Your Personality: On graduation day, you are the one who will be voted "most likely to succeed." You are a trollerific genius and tend to be a deep thinker.

Your Style: When it comes to fashion, you like stuff that's practical so that everything can mix and match. You do most of your shopping once a year, right before school starts. Your clothes would be best described as preppy.

SAPPHIRE

To Try: Invest in some accessories. A few colored bracelets or a sparkly necklace can add a personal touch to your daily outfits.

Hot to Shop!

Find out where each troll gets
her wardrobe essentials.

Amethyst

Her Style:
This supersweet troll
is girly-girl to the
core. Just like her
troll Chihuahua,
Amethyst's fave shade
is pink.

Her Wardrobe
Wish List:
A pair of Mary Janes,
anything with hearts
on it, a necklace with
an "A" written in
rhinestones, and a
pleated miniskirt.

Score Her Style:
You don't have to spend a
ton of cash to look head-to-
toe Amethyst. Just stock up on
pretty accents like barrettes,
sparkly jewelry, ankle socks,
and, of course, anything pink.

9

Topaz

Her Style:
While she may come across as a little bit kooky, this troll's got fabulous style. She's always the first to try a trend, and she's started a few herself.

Her Wardrobe Wish List:
A pair of bright yellow sneakers, cool sunglasses, a metallic bag, and a brightly colored sweater that's soft and fuzzy.

Score Her Style:
Get creative. Flip through magazines and pick out the styles you like best. Then try using the clothes you already have to put those looks together.

Onyx

Her Style:
This Goth troll loves stuff that's black and chunky—just check out those cool doodads she uses to keep her pigtails in place. Although her style can be dramatic, she's super sweet on the inside.

Her Wardrobe Wish List:
A studded belt, a ton of rubber bracelets, and lots of tights (black or purple, naturally!).

Score Her Style:
Hit a music store and snap up a T-shirt of your favorite band. Try pairing the shirt with a skirt, bright tights or kneesocks, and chunky boots. Dark nail polish and lip gloss can add to your funky look.

Ruby

Her Style:
Ruby is all about the spotlight! She shines in anything bright, from her hair-raising 'do to the bottoms of her platform shoes.

Her Wardrobe Wish List:
The coolest, most hi-tech sneakers, a pair of low-rise bootleg jeans, a necklace with a big star charm, and a pile of T-shirts in rainbow shades.

Score Her Style:
Hit all of your favorite stores at the mall to stock up on essentials like jeans and T-shirts. And make sure to take your friends along to get the thumbs-up on all of your purchases!

Sapphire

Her Style:
Sapphire is into the classics—so bring on the books, and all those cute and classically cut clothes.

Her Wardrobe Wish List:
A few white button-down shirts in different styles, Mary Janes, tennis socks with pom-poms on the heels, and an argyle sweater in pastel shades.

Score Her Style:
Keep it simple and stick to colors that work easily together (blue and purple or raspberry and lavender). Unique socks are a must, and layering is great, too.

Fashionista 101

*N*o matter what your latest look is, there are always a couple of ideas that never go out of style.

- **High-top sneakers:** These come in every color under the sun. They look just as cool with pants or a dress and are one of the few clothing items that won't look totally uncool if you and your BFFL both show up wearing the same pair.

- **Backpack:** Personalize it with buttons, drawings, or little charms you can hang off of the zipper. And make sure it has lots of secure sections for money, your school ID, and snacks! After all, no one wants banana all over her science homework!

- **Hair bands:** Braids, bunches, ponytails … the list goes on! Topaz can't leave home without 'em. Look for the ones without metal clasps so you can avoid snagging your strands.

- **Tanks and white T's:** These super cheap wardrobe pieces are a staple that never goes out of style (Ruby always has a bunch on hand.) They work with jeans or dressed up under a cute cardigan. These aren't expensive, so be sure yours are always looking chic and new!

- **Puffy jacket or vest:** Look cool and stay warm. Pick up one in a basic color like black or navy and it will work well with everything. Promise!

Listen up! For ideas on how to customize your basics, flip to page 30!

- **Button-down shirt:** Sapphire loves hers and says the secret is to buy one that's cut for a girl—a little slimmer in the shoulders and not as long as a guy's version.

- **A-line skirt:** This is a skirt that fits at the waist and then gently slopes out (if you lay it down flat, it almost looks like a triangle). This style is universally flattering, especially if the hem hits just above your knees.

- **Unique piece of jewelry:** Do you love hearts like Amethyst or stars like Ruby? It's always great to have one piece of jewelry that you can wear all the time. Choose something that can be dressy or casual. You can also make your own special piece of jewelry. Either way, whatever you choose will be your own little good luck charm!

Quiz: What's Your Fashion Passion?

*A*re you a natural wonder who likes back-to-basics duds like T's and denim, or are you more of a girly girl who loves miniskirts and makeup? Perhaps you're somewhere in between. Take this quiz to find your fashion passion, and get some tips on how to spark up your style.

1. **What do you do after school?**
   a. Cruise the mall
   b. Burn CDs on my computer
   c. My nails
   d. Walk my dog

2. **What's you favorite article of clothing?**
   a. Designer jeans
   b. Pink cardigan
   c. Vintage suede jacket
   d. Black boots

3. **How long does it take you to get ready for a party?**
   a. A couple of hours shopping for the perfect outfit
   b. An hour, plus phone time consulting with friends
   c. Not long—I wear my everyday clothes.
   d. Half an hour putting something interesting together

4. **What's your idea of a perfect Friday night?**
   a. Going out with a bunch of friends for pizza.
   b. Having my best friends over for a movie night
   c. Going to see a rock concert
   d. A spa night with my best bud

5. **What type of prom dress would you like?**
   a. I haven't even thought about it
   b. Something really glam that's red and strapless
   c. Probably something black or from a thrift store
   d. I'm going to be pretty in pink!

6. **How often do you go shopping for clothes?**
   a. I love to go shopping with my friends all the time.
   b. I'd rather go to a CD store.
   c. Whenever I need a new outfit
   d. Not often. I like my jeans broken-in and frayed.

7. **What is something you would never wear?**
   a. A sweatshirt
   b. A head-to-toe preppy look
   c. Anything black
   d. A white button-down shirt

8. **What would you wear if you were meeting your crush?**
   a. My favorite band T-shirt
   b. My lucky pink sweater
   c. My denim miniskirt
   d. My sparkly necklace

9. Yikes! You overslept. What's your emergency outfit?

    a. Black boots, pants, and a T-shirt
    b. Low-rider jeans and my favorite baby T
    c. A long skirt, flip-flops, and the T-shirt I slept in
    d. Jeans, a button-down, a cardigan, and ballet flats

10. What would you wear to a beach party?

    a. A bikini
    b. A bikini with a matching sarong
    c. Cutoffs and a bikini top
    d. Dark shorts and a white tank top

Your Score

	a)	b)	c)	d)
1.	3	2	1	0
2.	1	3	0	2
3.	1	3	2	0
4.	1	3	2	0
5.	0	1	2	3
6.	3	2	1	0
7.	1	2	3	0
8.	2	3	1	0
9.	2	1	0	3
10.	1	3	0	2

Your Fashion Passion

0-7 Boho Girl

You like eclectic clothes that feel good, and you aren't as concerned with the latest trends. You love to shop in thrift stores for unusual and fun clothes. Since you're daring when it comes to clothes, why not try crafting some of your own?

8-15 Glam Girl

When it comes to clothes, you are a true fashionista. You like nothing better than spending hours poring over fashion magazines to get ideas for outfits to check out the next time you're taking a troll stroll through the mall. Just make sure you don't get too stuck in the trends—a true fashionista knows that she should always have some classic pieces to balance her funky trend items. That way you won't have to buy a whole new wardrobe every few months!

16-22 Rocker Girl

First comes music, then comes fashion. When you like a band, you buy their T-shirt as well as their latest CD. Your look is pretty simple since you almost always wear jeans and sneakers or boots. While you prefer to wear black, don't get stuck in a style rut. Why not mix it up by wearing a denim skirt or cool, colorful cords instead of jeans? And don't be afraid of necklaces, and hair accessories—they're the easiest way to add a personal stamp to any outfit.

23-30 Girly Girl

When it comes to style, yours is purely pretty. Your closet is super organized and full of lots of pink, yellow, and lavender clothes. You like your outfits to match, so all of those cardigans with the matching tank tops are a wardrobe must. You're equally comfortable in jeans or skirts, and you love busting out all of your pretty sundresses in the summer. You definitely have your style down, but don't be afraid to take a walk on the wild side with a funky bag, hip wedge sandals, or even a pair of dangly earrings.

Sapphire's Shopping 411

*W*anna hit the mall like a master, be a diva in the drugstore, or find the most super stuff at a sale? No prob. Check out Sapphire's smart and easy tips on cruising the stores with some real savvy.

* **Do** wear comfy clothing. The best things to wear are clothes that fit snuggly (think tank tops and leggings) so you can try stuff on over them. This way you can try on all your loot at once instead of constantly waiting in lines for dressing rooms.

* **Don't** buy something just because it's on sale. Ask yourself, "Would I buy this if it were full price?" If the answer is no, it will just end up hanging in your closet, and that super-cheap bargain will be a waste of money.

* **Do** shop with a best bud. Sometimes it's hard to see if something fits you properly, especially from the back.

Don't be a total top-to-toe trendmeister. Just because metallics are in doesn't mean you have to become a walking piece of tinfoil. Since trends usually don't last long, buy one piece (a belt, a bag, or some shoes) and just mix it in with your regular clothes.

Do stock up on basics. Find out which brand makes the most flattering basics for your body type. When they go on sale, buy 'em in bulk—you'll always use T's, tanks, socks, and underwear. And spread the word! Maybe this Christmas, Grandma will get you something you'll actually wear instead of another Santa sweater.

Don't think that just because it looks good on your best bud, it will work on you. Everyone has different coloring and different body types.

Do check online. Most big chain stores have Web sites, so it's easy to log on and browse for sales before you hit the mall. But remember to ask an adult for permission before you actually purchase anything online.

Don't go in unprepared. If you're shopping for back to school, make a list of the items of clothing that you really need. No one wants to end up with five sweaters and no bottoms!

Do experiment. Why not try on a bunch of things until you find something you really like? It's free to look, and you might be surprised by what you end up choosing.

Jean Genius!

Who doesn't love denim? The only problem is, with so many different styles, washes, and cuts to choose from, finding the perfect pair can be more than a little tricky. Well, jean-styling Ruby (she likes hers with big, chunky cuffs) has the lowdown on how to pick your perfect blues.

Straight Leg

These jeans go out at the hips a little bit and then fall straight down.

Ruby says: These are great for tomboy types and not the most flattering on curvy girls. I think these look killer with big boots!

Boot Cut

These go out a bit at the hips, taper at the knee, and then flare out a little from the knee down to the ankle. They look great on curvy shapes.

Ruby says: Totally cool! This style flatters almost every body type. I like mine when the waistband hits just below my belly button.

Tapered Leg

These jeans look totally retro cool. They are a slim cut from the waist all the way down to the ankle. Get them a tad long so they bunch a bit at the ankles. These look awesome on tall, slim figures.

Ruby says: If you're a cuffer like me, these are the best because the cuff totally stays put. I love to wear mine with cute flat shoes.

Reverse Fit

These are wider in the hips and then get slimmer as they go down toward the ankle.

Ruby says: If you like your jeans a touch baggy but still want them to be flattering, this is a great fit—if jeans are wide all the way down, you might look like a clown!

Stretch

This means that the jeans are made with Lycra and have some give to them.

Ruby says: Stretch jeans are the bomb! They flatter every shape because they fit your body perfectly, and they're also super comfy (even after two slices of pizza!).

Bad Trend Alert

Just because your favorite celebrity wears something on the red carpet doesn't mean it will work on you. Remember, these people get dressed to be photographed, not to go to math class. Below, the trollz girls have rounded up some "don't go there" fashion tips, along with some ideas on what to do instead.

Too Color-coded

Purple may be the color of the moment, but that doesn't mean you should wear a purple top, skirt, and sneakers. Take a tip from Ruby, who always offsets her bright red hair with contrasting colors. Unless it's a basic black dress with some dainty flats, wearing all one color is a no-no.

Too Many Patterns

Take inspiration from Sapphire. She loves to pair a checked mini with a perky solid-colored shirt and sweater set that picks up the colors in the skirt. If you like a pattern, it's best to wear it on one item of clothing and pair it with solids.

Too Tight

Clothes that are too tight just don't look good. These days, each clothing company has a different idea of what each size looks like, so don't feel like you always have to buy the same size. It's more flattering (and comfortable) to have clothes that fit you well.

Too Much Skin

Just because pop stars wear super-short crop tops and miniskirts with way-high slits doesn't mean it's appropriate for the rest of us. Just ask Amethyst, who is all about looking pretty and girly. If you want to wear a miniskirt, cover up on top with a short-sleeved collared T-shirt. Likewise, team a tiny tank with a knee-length skirt or cool capris.

Too Much Bling

All your fave hip-hop and R&B stars may load up on the chains, rings, and giant watches, but it's too-too much in the real world. Accessories are supposed to complement your outfit, not overwhelm it. Fashion genius Topaz says if you're wearing big earrings, skip the necklace—and vice versa. Bracelets go with both, or try making one piece of jewelry that you really love your signature piece. (Check out Topaz's bejeweled headband for inspiration!)

Too Much Makeup

Even though Onyx likes her look dark and dramatic, she's always sure to keep her makeup from looking over-the-top. Don't wear heavy makeup on your eyes and lips at the same time. Pick either one and your look will always be cool.

Too Retro

We all love colorful clothes from the '80s and hippie styles from the '70s, but don't get too caught up in the flashback fever. If you slip into bell-bottoms, platforms, and a flower-power top, you'll look like you're off to a Halloween party. If you love a certain old-school style, pick a few key pieces and work them into your modern-day wardrobe.

Quiz: What's Up, Glam Girl?

*S*o you just found out that your friend is having a huge birthday bash in two weeks . . . and it's formal. What do you wear? Figure out what your dress-up style is by taking this quiz. It will make your hunt for the perfect outfit a whole lot easier!

1. **What's your idea of the perfect date?**
   a. Dinner and a movie
   b. Going to see a band
   c. A shared fudge brownie

2. **Are you romantic?**
   a. If I met the right guy...
   b. Totally!
   c. I guess so, but I'm shy to admit it.

3. **Who is your fave glam icon?**
   a. J. Lo
   b. Reese Witherspoon
   c. Gwen Stefani

4. **What do you want to be when you grow up?**
   a. A vet
   b. A fashion designer
   c. A VJ

26

5. What's in your purse on a Friday night?

a. Lip gloss and gum
b. Cell phone, lip gloss, perfume, and powder
c. A band to put my hair up and lip gloss

6. What's your idea of a perfect shopping day?

a. In and out in an hour
b. A credit card with my name on it
c. A couple of hours at the mall with my friends

7. How often do you get dressed up?

a. Only for the holidays
b. When I want to feel special
c. All the time

8. How many dresses do you own?

a. 10-15
b. 5-10
c. Less than 5

9. What type of magazines do you read?

a. Mainly music mags
b. Any fashion mag I can get my hands on
c. Anything with quizzes and lifestyle tips

10. What's you idea of the perfect party?

a. A slumber party
b. A massive beach bash
c. A medium-size get-together with good music

Your Score

1.	a) 0	b) 1	c) 2
2.	a) 1	b) 0	c) 2
3.	a) 0	b) 2	c) 1
4.	a) 2	b) 0	c) 1
5.	a) 2	b) 0	c) 1
6.	a) 1	b) 0	c) 2
7.	a) 1	b) 2	c) 0
8.	a) 0	b) 2	c) 1
9.	a) 1	b) 0	c) 2
10.	a) 2	b) 0	c) 1

Answers

0-7 points

Dress Type: A gown with sparkles or ruffles and matching shoes

What it says about you: You love nothing better than to get glam and stand out in a crowd. When it comes to color, you'll wear anything bright, like red, raspberry, or peacock blue. The best place for you to shop is a department store where there are racks and racks of dresses in every style—that way you can try on as many as you like.

Glam Tip: Why not try something classic, like a strapless top with a full skirt and some classy satin gloves for a totally '50s retro look?

8-14 points

Dress Type: A sleeveless to-the-knee dress with cute open-toed sandals

What it says about you: You're very feminine and pretty confident about your looks. You have a style that's simple and perky, and you love bright colors like pink, green, and yellow. You're a social butterfly, but you prefer to hang in a small group of five or six friends. When it comes to dress shopping, you're the type that needs to window shop before making a decision.

Glam Tip: Don't just limit yourself to a dress—these days there are scads of great skirts that you can team with pretty camisoles. This way you know that no one will show up wearing the same exact outfit!

15-20

Dress Type: A plain black skirt with a flowery shirt

What it says about you: You're interested in fashion and style, but don't always know where to start. Your attitude is always low-key and you have countless interests, so your weekends aren't usually spent at the mall. You'd rather be known for your brains than your new jeans. To help make shopping a bit easier, you should try browsing some online shopping sites (but check with an adult before you buy!). You can check out a bunch of party outfits without spending too much time in a store.

Glam Tip: An easy way to pick a dress is to think about what body part you like most. If your arms are muscular, go sleeveless. You like your legs? Go short. For great shoulders, try a halter neck.

She's Crafty

*P*art of personal style is putting your own creative stamp on stuff. Topaz is the master of making clothes look totally one-of-a-kind. You can also take a few basic pieces and funk them up with some snips and sewing tricks. Always ask an adult for permission before you put scissors to that brand-new shirt!

Cool-For-School Tank

Topaz says: "This is a basic tank that I've made look totally pretty with all the sparkles. It's so easy to do and the perfect gift for Amethyst!"

What You'll Need

◎ A basic white tank top
◎ Fabric glue
◎ A package of fake rhinestones
◎ A marker
◎ One foot of your favorite ribbon

Directions

1. Lay the tank top down flat and arrange the rhinestones into your desired pattern.
2. When your design looks how you want it, put a marker dot on the tank where each rhinestone is going to go.

3. Put a tiny dot of fabric glue on the marker dot and stick a stone down on the tank. If you are gluing onto both the front and back of the tank, do one side and then wait for the glue to dry before turning the tank over and finishing the other side.

4. Cut the ribbon in half and tie a bow at each shoulder. Trim the ends of the ribbon to the desired length.

Rocker Cuff

Topaz says: "Since Onyx and I have totally different tastes, it's not always easy for me to find something that she'll like. This punk rock cuff bracelet is a total winner!"

What You'll Need

◎ 10-inch strip of black vinyl (2 inches wide)
◎ 10-inch strip of red vinyl (1 inch wide)
◎ Fabric glue
◎ A small strip of Velcro
◎ Needle and a spool of black thread
◎ Silver marker

Directions

1. Lay the black vinyl strip on a flat surface. Lay the red strip on top of the black piece, centering it.

2. Take your needle and thread and stitch the red vinyl onto the black piece.

3. Take a one-inch square of Velcro and glue one side to one end of the black vinyl and the other side to the other end.

4. With the silver marker, write your message on the red vinyl. (Topaz wrote "Rock 'n' Roll Trollz" on the bracelet she made for Onyx.)

Tied Up to a T

Topaz says: "This is an awesome way to make an old T-shirt look totally new. Of all the trollz, I think Ruby would like this the best because it's a bold style statement."

What You'll Need

- One plain white crew neck T-shirt
- Scissors
- A marker
- A hole punch
- Three feet of ribbon in a bright color

Directions

1. Lay the T-shirt down flat. Grab the scissors and cut the sleeves off the shirt by following the seam that goes from the armpit up to the shoulder.
2. Take the marker and draw a line for the shoulder (by the neck) from either side and down the front so that your T-shirt can become a V-neck.
3. Cut along the marker line.
4. Cut along the seams that go from the armpits to the bottom of the T-shirt on either side.
5. Take the hole punch and make a line of holes (an inch apart) from the armpits to the bottom of the T-shirt on either side. Keep the last hole about half an inch from the bottom edge of the shirt. Make sure to punch the holes all the way through from the front panel of the shirt to the back.
6. Grab your ribbon and cut it in half.

7. Start threading the ribbon beginning from the top (just below the armpit) and working your way down. This is like lacing up your sneakers. When you get to the bottom, tie the ribbon into a bow and snip off any excess.

Funky Feet

Topaz says: "Sapphire spends way more time in the science lab than the mall, so I figured I'd make her something she'd really use—funky socks that will look cool poking out over the tops of her loafers."

What You'll Need

◎ One pair of socks in a solid color
◎ One pair of socks in a cool contrasting pattern
◎ Scissors
◎ Needle and thread
◎ Six small buttons in a fun color

How to Make It

1. Take the socks that you want to show the most and cut the ankle and toes off.

2. Slip these socks on top of the other pair and sew them down at the toes, the heel, and the ankle so that both pairs are completely attached.

3. Take three of the six buttons and sew them onto the top of one of the socks in whatever pattern you want (feel free to use more buttons).

4. Repeat the pattern on the second sock.

Quiz: Are You Stuck in a Style Rut?

*R*outine can be good, but when it comes to your wardrobe, the same old thing can get pretty boring. Take this quiz to find out if your closet could use a funky new attitude.

1. **You wear different jeans throughout the week.**
   a. true
   b. false

2. **None of your clothes are more than three years old.**
   a. true
   b. false

3. **Your hair looks totally different from the way it did three years ago.**
   a. true
   b. false

4. **You know what an A-line skirt is.**
   a. true
   b. false

5. **You've tossed out all of your camp T-shirts from two summers ago.**
   a. true
   b. false

6. You have a secret desire to be prom queen someday.
   a. true
   b. false

7. If your crush asked you out for tonight, you could pull together a cool outfit in five minutes.
   a. true
   b. false

8. People often copy the outfits that you put together.
   a. true
   b. false

9. Your little sister is always borrowing your clothes.
   a. true
   b. false

10. You think of what you're going to wear to school the night before.
    a. true
    b. false

Your Score

Mostly Trues: When it comes to personal style, you're pretty flexible. You're willing to try a few new trends, but you draw the line at some of the crazier ones. You feel confident in your outfit choices and know how to throw something cool together at the last minute. If you want ideas on how to change your look, check out the different outfits your fave star puts together for inspiration. Also, don't feel like you have to buy a whole new wardrobe every season. You can always update your look with a couple of tweaks and a few small purchases, like a hat, scarf, bag, or brooch.

Mostly Falses: While it can be great to get into a fashion groove, it might be time for a change if you've been in the same one since third grade. First, go through your closet and toss out anything that's stained or has holes in it. Next, put aside all the stuff that you haven't worn in more than a year and ask an adult if it's okay to donate it to a thrift store. Now, make a list of clothing items that you are missing—a nice pair of jeans, a denim jacket, a couple of cool T-shirts, and winter or summer skirts or pants. Don't feel like you have to buy everything at once—just keep the list tacked up on the wall in your bedroom and pick up some new piece whenever you have the time or the money. Another cool way to score some new wardrobe finds without spending a penny is to trade with friends. A top that you never wear might become a wardrobe staple for someone else.

Are you ready to get gorgeous?

*W*hen it comes to your looks, the quickest change you can make is with your makeup or hairstyle. After all, it takes two seconds to put on some lip gloss and only costs a couple of dollars. Since all the trollz have their own unique style, they also have their own beauty secrets. So, whether you want to know what type of haircut suits your face or how to paint on the perfect manicure, these next pages will have you covered! It will make your next shopping trip to buy beauty loot an absolute snap, and styling your strands will be oh-so-simple. It's time to put your best face forward.

Amethyst's Top Ten Must-Have Makeup Secrets

*A*re you ready for your close-up? You will be with these insider secrets and product pointers.

1. **Lotsa Lashes:** Curling your eyelashes is a great way to open up eyes without putting on any makeup. Grab an eyelash curler and hold it like a pair of scissors (using thumb and index finger). Looking straight ahead, place the curler so that your lashes sit between the two curling pads. Clamp the curler down on the lashes, count to ten, and let go.

2. **Pretty Pout:** For a lip look that's light, rub your index finger on your lipstick and then tap your finger onto your lips. The effect is that of a natural stain instead of a load of lipstick.

3. **Zit Tip:** A picked zit can take up to three times longer to go away than an unpicked one.

4. **Mascara Makeover:** Skip under-eye mascara smears by applying it to your top lashes only.

5. **No-brainer Blush:** Looking for a natural cheek color? Pick one that's similar to the crimson shade you turn when you get embarrassed.

6. **Lighten Up:** If you like to wear dark lipstick like Onyx, keep your eye makeup subtle—and vice versa. Lots of liner and mascara will look best with clear gloss. Playing up both features is total overload.

7. **Pucker Up:** Want to give your lips some sparkle? Take a light lip gloss that has a lot of shimmer to it and put a dot right in the middle of your lower lip. The sparkle reflects light and makes your lips look super shiny.

8. **The Big Cover-up:** If you have a breakout on your cheeks, don't use any face products (blush or powder) that have shimmer in them. This will only highlight your acne. Stick to powder-based products that are matte instead.

9. **Shine Buster:** Blotting paper is better than face powder for controlling a shiny T-zone (forehead, nose, and chin) because they absorb shine without caking on more powder. If you don't have any blotting paper on hand, peel apart a tissue so that you have two thin pieces. Use one of them to blot your face, and save the other one for later!

10. **Less Is More:** When deciding how much makeup to wear, don't feel that you have to use a truckload of products. Keep it simple by picking out the feature you like most on your face. Then highlight that one feature with one or two products.

Quiz: Are You a Skin Whiz?

*W*ho doesn't want a healthy glow? The first thing you need to do is figure out what type of skin you have. Take our quick quiz, add up the results, and then check out the answers to find out what you need to do for a smooth, flawless face.

1. **When you wake up in the morning, your skin looks:**
   a. Pretty good, but there's always the odd zit.
   b. Like one big flake-fest.
   c. Shiny enough to double as a mirror.

2. **If your skin were a fruit, what type would it be?**
   a. Smooth and soft as a peach
   b. Tight like an apple
   c. Like a strawberry with lots of visible pores

3. **When you wash your face with a cream cleanser, how does it feel when you're done?**
   a. Not too bad, but my nose is still a bit slick
   b. So dry I need to put on moisturizer right away
   c. Like I could wash it again and it still isn't clean

40

4. How often do you get zits?

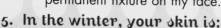

   a. Sometimes, and I always have a couple of blackheads on my nose.
   b. Not very often
   c. Are you kidding me? They're a permanent fixture on my face.

5. In the winter, your skin is:

   a. A little schizoid—sometimes dry and sometimes oily.
   b. Flaky, itchy, and often red.
   c. Oily, and the zits are still there.

6. What does your skin look like by lunchtime?

   a. My forehead and nose will be a little shiny.
   b. The exact same as it did in the morning
   c. I need to use blotting paper to get rid of the greasies.

7. How oily is your scalp?

   a. I can skip a shampoo once in a while.
   b. I can lather up every other day.
   c. I have to wash my hair every day, especially after sports.

8. After school, what would happen if you pressed a tissue to your face for five seconds and then held it up to the light?

   a. It would be almost transparent from my forehead and nose.
   b. There would be a small transparent spot from my nose.
   c. The tissue would be almost translucent.

Your Score

Mostly A's: You've got *combination skin* that's oily in the T-zone (forehead, nose, and chin) and normal to dry in the cheeks. You probably have a few blackheads and get a zit now and then.

Mostly B's: You've got *dry skin* that's probably also a tad sensitive. The only place you would ever get oily is around the nose.

Mostly C's: You've got *oily skin* with enlarged pores in the nose and cheek area, and you're also prone to frequent breakouts.

Combination Skin

If you've got this type of face, you're definitely not alone—it's by far the most common kind of skin for teens. The pores in your T-zone—forehead, nose, and chin—are oily, and your cheeks and neck are drier. In the areas where you're greasy, your pores are probably also larger, so they get clogged up with blackheads and whiteheads. To help control your T-zone without drying out your cheeks, you'll need products that remove surface oil but aren't too harsh. Try a light, milky cleanser, followed by an alcohol-free toner. Next, if your skin feels tight in certain parts, apply a dab of oil-free moisturizer. To keep your T-zone from getting shiny in the middle of the day, stash blotting papers in your bag.

Dry Skin

The trick with dry skin is to baby it and keep it moisturized, since it can feel sensitive and flaky a lot of the time. You don't want to use any products that are going to remove too much of the natural oils in the skin. Stay away from face products that lather up (like soaps and cleansing gels) since they contain detergents that are very harsh on dry skin. There are lots of gentle, non-foaming cleansers on the market today. If you want to do a toner, make sure it has no alcohol and put on cream as soon as you're done. Moisturizers absorb better when skin is still damp. To keep your pores clean and your face free of any flakes, you can also do a mild scrub twice a week before applying cream. But don't go crazy—and stop at the first sign of redness.

Oily Skin

If you've got this type of face, your pores are probably visible all over your face and you frequently break out in zits and blackheads. That's because your skin produces an excess of sebum (oil) that mixes with dead skin cells on your face to clog up your pores. The trick to controlling oily skin is to use a gel-based cleanser and an oil-controlling toner. If your skin doesn't feel tight when you're done with both of those, you should also just skip moisturizer altogether. Twice a week, clean your face with an anti-bacterial scrub, and always keep a spot treatment on hand for pesky whiteheads. If you love to do masks, try an exfoliating mask once a week. Look for one that contains clay (it will say so on the tube), since this is a great ingredient for soaking up excess oil.

Topaz's Ten Best Tress Tricks

$\mathcal{F}$or the trollz girls, it's all about the hair! For shiny, happy hair of your own, just follow Topaz's simple strand secrets.

1. **Shower Time:** If you wash your hair every day, try just sudsing up your scalp (where the greasies are) to avoid drying out your ends. And when you condition, just apply it on your tips—your roots don't need the added lube.

2. **Frizzies Be Gone:** Don't rub your wet head with a towel or knot it up genie style—it musses up your strands. Instead, grab a section of your hair in a towel and gently squeeze out the moisture. This will also help cut your combing time in half!

3. **Comb Clue:** Your hair is pretty sensitive, so be careful when combing. The best time to take out tangles is in the shower, using a wide-toothed comb. Always start combing the ends, slowly working your way up to the roots. This way you avoid tugging at any snags and snapping your strands.

4. **Product Overload:** Ever have a morning when you're a little heavy-handed with the pomade or wax? No prob. Just spritz your strands with an aerosol hairspray. The alcohol in the product will help absorb any excess oils.

5. **Va-va Volume:** If you want to add a little lift to your strands (just take a look at Topaz's golden poof!), use a volumizing spray. But be sure to apply it only on the roots—if you apply product all the way down the hair shaft, it will just weigh down your strands. The easiest way to apply it is to lift up a chunk of your hair with one hand and spritz the roots with the other.

6. **Parting Ways:** A side part is almost always more flattering than a middle one.

7. **Knot Free:** Avoid getting snags in your hair when pulling out your ponytail holder by coating the band with a tiny bit of conditioner beforehand. That way the holder glides out easily when you want it to.

8. **Straight Up:** If you're blow-drying your hair straight, always spritz damp hair with a leave-in conditioner beforehand so strands won't get fried.

9. **Bang-Up Job:** It doesn't matter what shape face you have—when cutting bangs, it's more flattering to have them sloping down a bit at the sides than cut straight across.

10. **Creative You:** Don't be afraid to experiment with your hair. Even if you don't want to cut it, you can still try lots of different styles with just a blow-dryer, some styling products, and hair accessories.

Score! Onyx's Guide to Beauty Loot

Finding the best products for your face and hair can be tricky. There's so much to choose from that it's easy to get overwhelmed. Just follow Onyx's guide and your next beauty shopping trip will be stress-free.

* **Do** make a list before you go. Otherwise it's easy to come back with a lip color that's the exact same shade as the one you already have.

* **Don't** buy something before trying it. If you're shopping at the drugstore and there's no tester, ask the salesperson if the store has a return policy. That way you can bring it back (with the receipt) if the color is totally different from what you thought. When it comes to lipstick, never put the tester on your lips. Instead, swipe a little bit onto your fingertip. This part is usually a little rosier than the rest of your finger so it's close to your natural lip color.

46

* **Do** ask for samples. If you're shopping at a department store, ask if you can take a small sample of the product home before you buy it. If not, ask her to apply some of the tester on your face so you can see how it looks.

* **Don't** buy any makeup without seeing what it looks like in natural outdoor light. Always go outside to see how a blush or foundation really looks on your skin.

* **Do** go with a friend. It's good to get a second opinion.

* **Don't** just pick a shampoo and conditioner because it smells good. While a sweet scent is important, there are hair-care products for all hair types. Check to see if a conditioner is for oily or normal hair. Is that gel frizz-fighting or volumizing? Take the time to read the package.

* **Do** be selective. You don't have to change your skincare routine all the time. If you're trying a new face product, give it a couple of weeks to see if it really works (unless you have an adverse reaction like stinging or redness).

* **Don't** think you have to use all products from one line. If you like one brand of cleanser and another brand of moisturizer, that's fine. Beauty products aren't like puzzle pieces that fit together—you can mix them up any way you want.

* **Do** some beauty spring cleaning. Products like mascara should be tossed every six months. All others are okay for about a year. The general rule is that if it smells funky or the color looks off, it's probably time to say bye-bye.

Your Perfect Haircut Guide

Two things determine your perfect haircut—the shape of your face and the texture of your tresses. Find yours below and you'll be ready for a new 'do—and a new you—in no time!

What's your face shape?

Heart This shape is wider at the temples and then tapers down to a small, round chin. Try some face-framing bangs (keep them long and blunt like Sapphire's). If you like to wear your hair on the shorter side, a bob that stops right at your jawbone would be perfect. If you hair is longer, add some layers to highlight your great cheekbones.

Round This shape often has full cheeks and a broad forehead. Make sure your hair always has a bit of volume at the top, so ask your stylist for some light layers around your face. If you love bangs, make sure your fringe always slopes downward at the edges. Bangs cut straight across are too severe and make the face look even rounder.

Square This shape has a prominent jawbone and great cheekbones. Your face looks just as pretty with a short pixie cut as it does with something longer. A flattering length for you would be an inch above your shoulders. If you feel that your face looks too angular, you can soften the look by parting your hair on the side.

Oval This shape has small, round cheeks and a rounded chin. This face shape can handle almost any haircut, from the shortest to the longest. If you have a small forehead, steer clear of bangs because they will just overpower your face. If you still want some hair around your face, ask your stylist to cut a couple of longer layers around your face.

What's your hair type?

Fine and Straight These tresses shouldn't be too long because they'll just look limp. A couple of layers around the face are okay, but always keep the ends and the rest of your hair cut fairly blunt. This will give the illusion of thicker hair.

Fine and Curly Lucky you! You have a pretty, natural wave to your strands. To accentuate the curls, get some long layers at jawbone level or lower all around your head. Add some light layers at the ends to add definition to your curls.

Thick and Straight This type of hair looks great cut at chin level or longer. If it's really thick and you cut it too short, your hair will look like a triangle! Thick hair can look really pretty cut very blunt, but if you feel you'd like your hair to look a little sleeker, ask your stylist to add some layers all around the ends of your hair.

Thick and Curly Unless you want to look like a basketball, don't cut your hair super short. Curly hair needs to have lots of layers in order to give your curls definition and keep them from looking frizzy. Keep your hair shoulder length or longer.

Trollz Beauty Patrol Q&A

*A*methyst, Topaz, Onyx, Ruby, and Sapphire are here to answer all of your nagging beauty questions.

Sun-kissed Trick

Q. I like to wear bronzer on my pale skin but it looks a little bit fake. What am I doing wrong?

Ruby: The trick to applying bronzer is to put it exactly where the sun hits your face when you're outside. Use a big powder brush to lightly dust some bronzing powder on your forehead, the middle of your cheeks, the tip of your nose, and your chin. A lot of bronzers have a shimmer to them. But the sparkles will highlight any blemishes you might have, so if you've got a breakout, try a formula that's shimmer-free.

Lip Service

Q. Why does my lipstick disappear an hour after I've put it on?

Onyx: Since I'm always wearing dark lipstick, I've totally mastered the art of getting mine to stick and not smear. First, apply a bit of concealer to your lips to create a base for the color to adhere to. Next, carefully line your lips along the natural lip line with a pencil that's the same as your natural lip color (don't go outside your lips—this always looks fake). Finally, apply a layer of lipstick, blot it with a tissue, and apply a final layer.

You're Blushing

Q. Where exactly does blush go on your cheeks?

Sapphire: I don't wear a pound of makeup, but blush is one of my favorites because it really brightens up my face. To figure out where your blush goes, look at yourself in the mirror and smile. The part of your cheeks that sticks out the most is where cheek color should be applied. Remember, when applying blush, use it sparingly.

Going Undercover

Q. What's the best way to conceal a zit so no one will notice it?

Topaz: Start with clean skin and grab a concealer that's fairly thick (formulation sticks are great). Take a small brush and dot some of the concealer right on the blemish. Then softly fan out the edges of the cover-up so it blends into your skin. Finally, dust on some loose powder to set the concealer. Don't keep applying powder throughout the day—it will just create a dry, flaky look that will be more obvious.

Straight Up

Q. How do I blow-dry my hair so it looks super straight and shiny?

Amethyst: First, apply a volumizing spray to the roots of damp hair. Do this by grabbing a section of the hair, pulling it up and spritzing right at the roots. Next, blow-dry hair by taking a one-inch square section and placing the brush on the underside, close to the roots. Point the nozzle of the blow-dryer in a downward direction, above the brush. Slowly pull the brush down toward the ends, moving the blow-dryer in the same direction at the same time. When your hair is dry, lightly spritz with a shine spray.

The Trollz' Favorite Beauty Booty

*S*ince each girl has such a unique style, she also has a totally unique makeup bag. Check out what Amethyst, Onyx, Topaz, Ruby, and Sapphire can't live without when it comes to their hair, face, and nails.

Amethyst

Beauty Philosophy: I want to feel pretty and good about myself every day, and show the world my best smile.

Her Favorite Things: Since my fave color is pink, it's no surprise that I love raspberry lip gloss. I don't like to wear too much makeup but I always give myself a manicure and paint on pink polish. When it comes to my hair, I get it trimmed every two months because I never want to have split ends. Also, once a week I'll put a deep conditioning treatment on my locks to keep them really shiny.

Onyx

Beauty Philosophy: No one else has the same look as me because I don't follow the trends.

Her Favorite Things: I always wear tons of black mascara and will sometimes wear black liquid eyeliner along my top lash line because it looks really cool. For my lipstick, I use a black eyeliner to line my lips and then I apply the darkest lipstick that I can find.

Topaz

Beauty Philosophy: I'm always trying something new, whether it's a certain hairstyle or a new product.

Her Favorite Things: My makeup bag is totally massive and I have to clean it out a lot because I love trying tons of different stuff. I always like to look kind of girly, so my favorite stuff is lipstick, pink blush, and different-colored mascaras (plum, blue, and green are totally awesome!)

Ruby

Beauty Philosophy: I like my hair to be bigger and my lips to be brighter than everyone else's.

Her Favorite Things: I always use loads of hairspray to keep my hair standing straight up like the total star that I am! I like my lips to be the same as my name—ruby red. Onyx taught me her trick to making her lipstick last, so now I always wear lip liner to keep mine in place.

Sapphire

Beauty Philosophy: I like to look perfectly polished, and I try to keep my makeup routine simple and healthy.

Her Favorite Things: Ever since Amethyst gave me a quick makeup lesson, I've been wearing pink lipstick, which is now my favorite. I also have a total weakness for yummy-smelling body lotions and bubble baths. After a hard day of studying, it's totally relaxing to have a good soak.

53

You've Got Nail

*W*ant to do the ultimate manicure and pedicure? Follow these six soaking, scrubbing, and softening steps, and your digits and piggies will be prepped and polished in no time.

1. **File Away:** Always file your toenails straight across, and your fingernails in a square with slightly rounded edges. When filing, don't go back and forth—that can make nails split. Instead, always keep the file going in one direction, toward the middle, by dragging across the nail edge, lifting it up, and then going back to the starting point.

2. **Super Soaker:** Fill up a basin or the bottom of your tub with water and dump in a cup of bath salts. Soak hands and feet for five minutes to help soften up tough skin and get 'em ready to be scrubbed.

3. **The Nitty Gritty:** Next, you need to remove all those rough spots (this is mainly for the feet but it also feels great on hands). Sit on the edge of the tub and put a dollop of a scrub in your hands. Cover your foot in it and massage in circular motions. You'll get a stress-relieving foot massage and you'll also ditch dry skin and flakes. Do the same with your hands.

4. Bye-bye Dry Spots: Now that your skin is smooth, take a cuticle cream or oil and apply it liberally around the edge of your nails so that it overlaps onto the skin. Let it sit for a minute and then push your cuticles back using an orange stick.

5. Soft and Smooth: The final step to perfect hands and feet is a great cream. Pick one that's really rich, and smooth it all over hands and feet (pop on some cotton socks and it will really sink into your piggies).

6. Perfect Painting: Always start by applying a layer of base (especially if you like dark polishes) because without it the colors can stain your nails. Next, apply two coats of your polish (wait a couple of minutes between coats) followed by a thin layer of topcoat to add a megawatt shine.

Quiz: Are You a Beauty Chameleon?

*D*o you change your looks every day or every year? While it's great to find a style and stick to it, there's always room for new tips, trends, and products. A little experimentation every now and again is great, and the genius of makeup is that you can wash it off! So, answer these questions and find out if you're on top of the trends.

1. **How many bottles of fragrance do you own?**
   a) five
   b) three
   c) one

2. **If you got a last-minute invite to a party, how easy would it be for you to get ready?**
   a) No time—I'd swap my scuffed jeans for nice ones.
   b) I can do a total makeover in no time!
   c) I'd make some tiny changes, like changing my shoes and hairdo.

3. **How often do you buy new products?**
   a) Every couple of months
   b) Whenever I run out of something
   c) I pick up a little something here and there.

4. If the trollz could create a magic beauty product for you, what would it be?

a) A lipstick that changes color every day
b) A magic cover-up that makes all my zits disappear
c) A spray that would clean my hair so I could skip the shower and sleep in longer in the morning

5. What makeup look would you never wear?

a) Red eye shadow
b) Anything too bright
c) I haven't met a beauty product I didn't like!

6. Are you the first of your friends to try out a new trend?

a) All the time
b) I wait until a few of my friends have road-tested a look.
c) Depends on the trend—if I like it, I'll try it.

7. What beauty product do you have way too much of?

a) Lip balm, because I always misplace it
b) I have a few shimmery lip glosses that I like to rotate.
c) Nail polish. I think I have about 30 bottles.

8. How many different styles can you create with your hair?

a) I can blow it straight and do a chic updo.
b) One—a ponytail
c) I'm always practicing new style ideas.

9. **What kind of makeup bag do you own?**
   a) I keep my stuff in a tiny pocket in my backpack.
   b) A big, colorful zip-up bag that's always full
   c) A small, cute bag that I can fit the necessities into

10. **Do you know how to use a straightening iron?**
    a) Of course!
    b) No way!
    c) I'm sure I'd figure it out.

Your Score:

1.	a) 2	b) 1	c) 0
2.	a) 0	b) 2	c) 1
3.	a) 1	b) 0	c) 2
4.	a) 2	b) 1	c) 0
5.	a) 1	b) 0	c) 2
6.	a) 2	b) 0	c) 1
7.	a) 0	b) 1	c) 2
8.	a) 1	b) 0	c) 2
9.	a) 0	b) 2	c) 1
10.	a) 2	b) 0	c) 1

Answers

0-7 Playing it Safe

You still feel a little intimidated when it comes to trying all the new beauty trends that appear in magazines and on red carpets.

What to try: Makeup-wise, it's easy to do something small, such as change your lipstick shade or switch from a black eyeliner to a softer brown. When it comes to

your haircut, ask your stylist if she could make a small change to your style. And after your stylist is done snipping, ask her to recommend a new product—a little gel or pomade can help you to create a whole new do.

8-14 Ready For a Few Changes

You are intrigued by hair products and makeup, but often feel overwhelmed by the number of choices. The trick to changing without looking like you've tried too hard is to stay within your comfort zone. Go through a bunch of magazines and find a photo of someone who shares your coloring and style sense. See how they tweak their look for different occasions.

What to try: Do you always wear mascara? Crank up your glam factor by trying a liner pencil in a darker shade (gray, brown, or navy) as well. To apply, just make small dots right at the base of the lashes—this makes them look really thick.

15-20 Total Chameleon

You are a total quick-change artist when it comes to your looks. One minute you're all glammed up and the next you're sporting a rocker vibe. You've realized that makeup and hair are a great way to show the world what kind of mood you're in.

What to try: You need to play it safe with certain products. When it comes to foundation and concealer, finding one that matches your skin perfectly can take some time. Also, with all the makeup experimentation you do, make sure that you have a good cleanser to wash it off thoroughly before you go to bed. Remember that the best beauty look is good skin!

Beauty Tool School

*I*n addition to knowing what products work for you, it's also important to know what tools you need to use when styling your strands and applying your makeup. Here's a list of what every girl should have.

Blush Brush: A good cheek-color brush can make your blusher go on more smoothly and more evenly. (You don't want to look like you have racing stripes on your cheeks!) Use a medium-size brush with round, fluffy bristles to really pick up the color.

Tip: *To make sure you don't apply too much cheek color at once, get some powder on the brush and tap the handle against your wrist. All the excess powder will fall off and not end up on your cheek.*

Powder Brush: This is the biggest of all the makeup brushes. It's great for applying sheer face powder or bronzer in the summertime. When using it, start by swiping your forehead, then swipe down your nose, your chin, and your cheeks.

Tip: *If you like to take a powder brush with you throughout the day, buy one that has a short handle so that it can easily fit inside your makeup bag. Leaving it loose in your regular bag or backpack can mess up the bristles and cover them in grime.*

Eyeliner Brush: There are loads of eye makeup brushes out there, but this is the easiest and the most useful. You can use it like an eyeliner by wetting the bristles and adding a touch of eye shadow powder. This gives a less harsh look than using a pencil. You can also use the brush dry to blend shadows or pencils.

Tip: *Remember to wash your brushes once a week in warm soapy water and then lay them out on a paper towel to dry. Not only is this hygienic, but it will also get rid of all the color that can muddy up your brush.*

Tweezers: These are for plucking any excess hairs away. Look for tweezers that have slanted tips because they make it easier to grab onto hairs.

Tip: *Never get tweezer-happy on your own. If you over-pluck your eyebrows, the hair can take a while to grow back, or it may not grow back at all! If you think your eyebrows are way too bushy, go to a professional to have them plucked or waxed.*

Blow-dryer: If you want your hair to look like a pro did it, you have to have a good blow-dryer. Look for one that has at least two different settings—cool and hot.

Tip: *If you have your hair up in curlers for a big event, always give them a blast with cool air before you take them out. The cool air helps to lock in the curl so it will last longer.*

Round Brush: If you want to blow-dry your hair straight, you're going to need a round brush. It's easier to handle than a paddle brush (one with a flat head) because it can be placed really close to the scalp when you're drying.

Tip: *If you ever want to give your ends a flip, just roll up sections of your hair and give them a quick blast with the blow-dryer.*

Pretty on the Inside

*O*kay, now that you've made your way through this whole book, remember that the most important beauty secret of all is your sparkling personality and magnetic smile. Your appearance is always a reflection of how you feel on the inside. So in addition to glossing, spritzing, and shopping, make sure you take care of yourself in other ways. Get tons of pillow time (they don't call it beauty sleep for nothing), eat right, enjoy exercise, and be happy! Every troll knows that all the magic or makeup in the world won't change how she really feels about herself on the inside. For that, you need to love yourself and have a close circle of good friends. And once you've got all that, a little lip gloss never hurts!